"Can you read the big words for me, Grandad?" asked Jenny.
Grandad put on his glasses, the kind that made writing clear,
but everything else rather **blurry**.

"150 grams of **butter**," he read.

He peered round.
"Now, where's that butter...?"

"What's next?" asked Jenny, scooping it into the bowl.

"150 grams of **flour**," read Grandad.

OH NO! Grandad grabbed...

ICING SUGAR

...the icing sugar!

White clouds flew everywhere.
"**Oops!**" giggled Jenny.

Once Grandad had cleaned his glasses,
he reached for the recipe book.
"Now, 200 grams of **carrots**.

Yummy! Let's get digging..."

Jenny looked round the garden.
"How funny having vegetables in a cake!
Imagine a brussels sprout cake...or a cabbage cake!"
"No, thank you!" laughed Grandad. "I'll stick to carrot cake any day –
and ours is going to be the tastiest cake ever!"

Grandad and Jenny washed the carrots
and added them to the mixture, but...

OH NO! They
forgot to chop them!
"Oh dear," said Jenny, "it doesn't look quite right."
"We haven't stirred it yet!" said Grandad.
Jenny stirred and stirred.

"Next," said Grandad, "we need **walnuts**,
then **eggs** and **caster sugar**
and a teaspoon of **cinnamon**."

"Walnuts first..."

OH NO!
They went in whole!

"Eggs next..."

OH NO!
Shells and all!

"Here's the sugar..."

OH NO!
Grandad reached for
the salt!

"Can't see anything
wrong with that now,"
said Grandad. "Can you?"

With Grandad's help, Jenny poured the mixture into two tins and then watched as Grandad put them carefully into the oven.

Jenny couldn't wait for the cake to be cooked.
Mummy was going to love it!

Finally the cake was done.
"OH NO!" said Jenny, "it doesn't look quite right!"
They each tried a crumb.
"OH NO!" said Grandad, "it doesn't taste quite right!
But we followed the recipe EXACTLY..."

"We forgot the cinna-thingy, that's why!" cried Jenny.
"And Mummy will be back any moment!

QUICK!
Let's hide the cake...

"in the garden!"

When Mummy came in, Jenny was quiet.
"What's wrong, Jenny?" asked Mummy.
"We were making a birthday surprise for you,"
said Jenny. "But it's a

catastrophe!"

And she led Mummy
out to the garden . . .

which was full of
beautiful birds!
"You've invited the birds – how clever you are!"
said Mummy. "This is the
best birthday surprise EVER!"

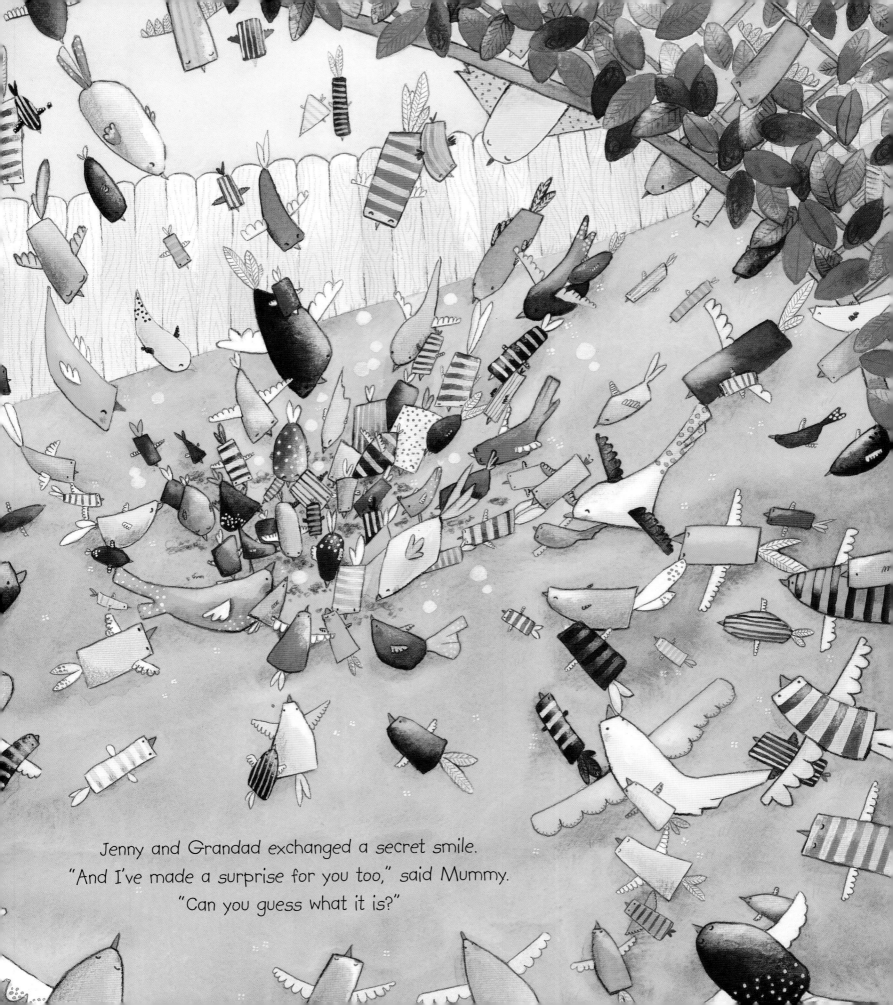

Jenny and Grandad exchanged a secret smile.
"And I've made a surprise for you too," said Mummy.
"Can you guess what it is?"

"It's a carrot cake!"
cried Jenny.
"It's a good job we gave ours to
the birds," Grandad whispered.

"Who wants a slice?" asked Mummy.
"I do!" cried Jenny and Grandad.
"Happy birthday!"

For my daughter, Jenny,
and her Grandad, Charles,
with much love

E.D.

For Grandad Joe and Nan Winnie,
who I know will be smiling down at
the catastrophe that this cake is

G.R.

First published in Great Britain in 2012 by

Gullane Children's Books
185 Fleet Street, London, EC4A 2HS
www.gullanebooks.com

10   9   8   7   6   5   4   3   2   1

Text © Elizabeth Dale 2012
Illustrations © Gemma Raynor 2012

The right of Elizabeth Dale and Gemma Raynor to be identified as
the author and illustrator of this work has been asserted by them
in accordance with the Copyright, Designs and Patents Act, 1988.
A CIP record for this title is available from the British Library.

ISBN: 978-1-86233-827-2

Printed and bound in China